LAZARUS

———

THE GENTLEMAN FROM
SAN FRANCISCO

LAZARUS

By LEONID ANDREYEV

———

The Gentleman from San Francisco

By IVAN BUNIN

Translated by

ABRAHAM YARMOLINSKY

Fredonia Books

Amsterdam, The Netherlands

Lazarus
by Leonid Andreyev

The Gentleman from San Francisco
by Ivan Bunin

ISBN: 1-4101-0429-X

Reprinted from the 1918 edition

Fredonia Books
Amsterdam, The Netherlands
http://www.fredoniabooks.com

In order to make original editions of historical works available to scholars at an economical price, this facsimile of the original edition of 1918 is reproduced from the best available copy and has been digitally enhanced to improve legibility, but the text remains unaltered to retain historical authenticity.

Foreword

Lazarus and *The Gentleman from San Francisco,* while fairly typical of Slavic literature, nevertheless contain few of the elements popularly associated with the work of contemporary Russian writers. They have no sex interest, no photographic descriptions of sordid conditions and no lugubrious philosophizing. These stories are not cheerful, yet their sadness is uplifting rather than depressing. They both contain what the Greek called *katharsis* in their tragedies,—that cleansing atmosphere which purges us of every baser feeling as we read them.

In *Lazarus* Andreyev has come as near as it is humanly possible to achieving the impossible. He has made concretely vivid an abstraction; he has arrested for an instant the ceaseless, unmeasurable flood of eternity; he has enclosed in a small frame the boundless void of the infinite. That which no human faculty can understand Andreyev has made almost intelligible. For a terrible moment he unveils the the secrets of the grave, and together with Augustus and the others who have come under the spell of Lazarus' eyes, we see how the most enduring of human monuments crumble into chaos even at the instant when they are being built, how nations upon nations tower like the shadows of silent ghosts, rising out of nothingness and sinking instantaneously into nothingness again, ''for Time was no more, and the beginning of all things came near their end: the building was still being built, and the builders were still hammering away, and its ruins were already seen and the void in its place; the man was still being born, but already funeral candles were burning at his head, and now they were extinguished, and there was the void in place of the man and of the funeral candles. And wrapped by void and darkness the man in despair trembled in the face of the Horror of the Infinite.''

FOREWORD

Lazarus is a story which depicts the misery of knowing the Unknowable.

In *The Gentleman from San Francisco* — Ivan Bunin demonstrates the poverty of wealth and the impotence of power. This story has been called the best work of fiction produced in Russia during the last decade.

The petty seriousness of the life of the modern Babylon, the deference paid by all people to bald heads and patent leather shoes and well-filled pockets, and the utter disregard for human feelings, are pictured with the pen of one who pities rather than scorns the frailties of the earth. The author stands aside, letting the world rush by like a hurdy gurdy, each gentleman from San Francisco or Boston or Berlin or Hong Kong sitting on his hobby horse, while the head waiter Luigi clownishly mocks their antics and nudges Death in the ribs.

The Gentleman from San Francisco shows the wide gulf that yawns between our estimate of our own worth and our actual worth. "I need the whole wide world for my amusement!" cries the man of wealth. "Yes, and here it is," answered Death, handing him a coffin. And as a further humiliation, those who were most anxious to serve this man of wealth in life are the first to shove the coffin into the ground.

The two stories in this book will arouse thought. They will be severely criticized by those who hate thought and as an excuse for their superficial shallowness condemn all Russian literature, for Russian literature is nothing if not thought-provoking. I do hope, however, that nobody will be found quite so devoid of a sense of humor as an admirable college dean and a sweet old lady the former of whom wrote to me that Chekhov's *Nine Humorous Tales* was immoral, and the latter of whom insisted that *Lazarus* was ungodly, inasmuch as Christ would never have raised a man from the dead for the purpose of teaching us so sad a lesson about the grave.

H. T. S.

CONTENTS

Lazarus

By Leonid Andreyev

TRANSLATED BY ABRAHAM YARMOLINSKY

I

WHEN Lazarus left the grave, where, for three days and three nights he had been under the enigmatical sway of death, and returned alive to his dwelling, for a long time no one noticed in him those sinister oddities, which, as time went on, made his very name a terror. Gladdened unspeakably by the sight of him who had been returned to life, those near to him carressed him unceasingly, and satiated their burning desire to serve him, in solicitude for his food and drink and garments. And they dressed him gorgeously, in bright colors of hope and laughter, and when, like to a bridegroom in his bridal vestures, he sat again among them at the table, and again ate and drank, they wept, overwhelmed with tenderness. And they summoned the neighbors to look at him who had risen miraculously from the dead. These came and shared the serene joy of the hosts. Strangers from far-off towns and hamlets came and adored the miracle in tempestuous words. Like to a beehive was the house of Mary and Martha.

Whatever was found new in Lazarus' face and gestures was thought to be some trace of a grave illness and of the shocks recently experienced. Evidently, the destruction wrought by death on the corpse was only arrested by the miraculous power, but its effects were still apparent; and what death had succeeded in doing with Lazarus' face and body, was like an artist's unfinished sketch seen under thin glass. On Lazarus' temples, under his eyes, and in the hollows of his cheeks, lay a deep and cadaverous blueness; cadaverously blue also were his long fingers, and around his fingernails, grown long in the grave, the blue had become purple and dark. On his lips the skin, swollen in the grave, had burst in places, and thin, reddish cracks were formed, shining as though covered with transparent mica. And he had grown stout. His body, puffed up in the grave, retained its monstrous size and showed those frightful swellings, in which one sensed the presence of the rank liquid of decomposition. But the heavy corpse-like odor which penetrated Lazarus' graveclothes and, it seemed, his very body, soon entirely disappeared, the blue spots on his face and hands grew paler, and the reddish cracks closed up, although they never disappeared altogether. That is how Lazarus looked when he appeared before people, in his second life, but his face looked natural to those who had seen him in the coffin.

In addition to the changes in his appearance, Lazarus' temper seemed to have undergone a transformation, but this circumstance startled no one and attracted no attention. Before his death Lazarus had always been cheerful and carefree, fond of laughter and a merry joke. It was because of this brightness and cheerfulness, with not a touch of malice and darkness, that the Master had grown so fond of him. But now Lazarus had grown grave and taciturn, he never jested, himself, nor responded with laughter to other people's jokes; and the words which he uttered, very infrequently, were the plainest, most ordinary and necessary words, as deprived of depth and significance, as those sounds with which animals express pain and pleasure, thirst and hunger. They were the words that one can say all one's life, and yet they give no indication of what pains and gladdens the depths of the soul.

Thus, with the face of a corpse which for three days had been under the heavy sway of death, dark and taciturn, already appallingly transformed, but still unrecognized by any one in his new self, he was sitting at the feasting table, among friends and relatives, and his gorgeous nuptial garments glittered with yellow gold and bloody scarlet. Broad waves of jubilation, now soft, now tempestuously-sonorous surged around him; warm glances of love were reaching out for his face, still cold with the coldness of the grave; and a friend's warm palm caressed his blue, heavy hand. And music played: the tympanum and the pipe, the cithara and the harp. It was as though bees hummed, grasshoppers chirped and birds warbled over the happy house of Mary and Martha.

II

One of the guests uncautiously lifted the veil. By a thoughtless word he broke the serene charm and uncovered the truth in all its naked ugliness. Ere the thought formed itself in his mind, his lips uttered with a smile:

"Why dost thou not tell us what happened yonder?"

And all grew silent, startled by the question. It was as if it occurred to them only now that for three days Lazarus had been dead, and they looked at him, anxiously awaiting his answer. But Lazarus kept silence.

"Thou dost not wish to tell us,"—wondered the man, "is it so terrible yonder?"

And again his thought came after his words. Had it been otherwise, he would not have asked this question, which at that very moment oppressed his heart with its insufferable horror. Uneasiness seized all present, and with a feeling of heavy weariness they awaited Lazarus' words, but he was silent, sternly and coldly, and his eyes were lowered. And as if for the first time, they noticed the frightful blueness of his face and his repulsive obesity. On the table, as though forgotten by Lazarus, rested his bluish-purple wrist, and to this all eyes turned, as if it were from it that the awaited answer was to come. The musicians were still playing, but now the silence reached them too, and even as water extinguishes scattered embers, so were their merry tunes extinguished in the silence. The pipe grew silent; the

voices of the sonorous tympanum and the murmuring harp died
away; and as if the strings had burst, the cithara answered with
a tremulous, broken note. Silence.

"Thou dost not wish to say?" repeated the guest, unable to
check his chattering tongue. But the stillness remained unbrok-
en, and the bluish-purple hand rested motionless. And then he
stirred slightly and everyone felt relieved. He lifted up his
eyes, and, lo! straightway embracing everything in one heavy
glance, fraught with weariness and horror, he looked at them,—
Lazarus who had arisen from the dead.

It was the third day since Lazarus had left the grave. Ever
since then many had experienced the pernicious power of his eye,
but neither those who were crushed by it forever, nor those who
found the strength to resist in it the primordial sources of life,—
which is as mysterious as death,—never could they explain the
horror which lay motionless in the depth of his black pupils.
Lazarus looked calmly and simply with no desire to conceal anything, but also with no intention to say anything; he looked
coldly, as he who is infinitely indifferent to those alive. Many
carefree people came close to him without noticing him, and only
later did they learn with astonishment and fear who that calm
stout man was, that walked slowly by, almost touching them with
his gorgeous and dazzling garments. The sun did not cease shining, when he was looking, nor did the fountain hush its murmur,
and the sky overhead remained cloudless and blue. But the man
under the spell of his enigmatical look heard no more the fountain and saw not the sky overhead. Sometimes, he wept bitterly,
sometimes he tore his hair and in frenzy called for help; but more
often it came to pass that apathetically and quietly he began to
die, and so he languished many years, before everybody's very
eyes, wasted away, colorless, flabby, dull, like a tree, silently
drying up in a stony soil. And of those who gazed at him, the
ones who wept madly, sometimes felt again the stir of life; the
others never.

"So thou dost not wish to tell us what thou hast seen yonder?" repeated the man. But now his voice was impassive and dull, and deadly gray weariness showed in Lazarus' eyes. And deadly, gray weariness covered like dust all the faces, and with dull amazement the guests stared at each other and did not understand wherefore they had gathered here and sat at the rich table. The talk ceased. They thought it was time to go home, but could not overcome the flaccid lazy weariness, which glued their muscles, and they kept on sitting there, yet apart and torn away from each other, like pale fires scattered over a dark field.

But the musicians were paid to play and again they took to their instruments, and again tunes full of studied mirth and studied sorrow began to flow and to rise. They unfolded the customary melody, but the guests hearkened in dull amazement. Already they knew not wherefore is it necessary, and why is it well, that people should pluck strings, inflate their cheeks, blow in thin pipes and produce a bizarre, many-voiced noise.

"What bad music,"—said someone.

The musicians took offense and left. Following them, the guests left one after another, for night was already come. And when placid darkness encircled them and they began to breathe with more ease, suddenly Lazarus' image loomed up before each one in formidable radiance: the blue face of a corpse, grave-clothes gorgeous and resplendent, a cold look, in the depths of which lay motionless an unknown horror. As though petrified, they were standing far apart, and darkness enveloped them, but in the darkness blazed brighter and brighter the super-natural vision of him who for three days had been under the enigmatical sway of death. For three days had he been dead: thrice had the sun risen and set, but he had been dead; children had played, streams murmured over pebbles, the wayfarer had lifted up hot dust in the highroad,—but he had been dead. And now he is again among them,—touches them,—looks at them,—looks at them! and through the black discs of his pupils, as through darkened glass, stares the unknowable Yonder.

III

No one was taking care of Lazarus, for no friends, no relatives were left to him, and the great desert, which encircled the
holy city, came near the very threshold of his dwelling. And the
desert entered his house, and stretched on his couch, like a wife,
and extinguished the fires. No one was taking care of Lazarus.
One after the other, his sisters—Mary and Martha—forsook
him. For a long while Martha was loath to abandon him, for
she knew not who would feed him and pity him, she wept and
prayed. But one night, when the wind was roaming in the desert and with a hissing sound the cypresses were bending over
the roof, she dressed noiselessly and secretly left the house.
Lazarus probably heard the door slam; it banged against the
side-post under the gusts of the desert wind, but he did not rise
to go out and to look at her that was abandoning him. All the
night long the cypresses hissed over his head and plaintively
thumped the door, letting in the cold, greedy desert.

Like a leper he was shunned by everyone, and it was pro-
posed to tie a bell to his neck, as is done with lepers, to warn
people against sudden meetings. But someone remarked, growing frightfully pale, that it would be too horrible if by night the
moaning of Lazarus' bell were suddenly heard under the
windows,—and so the project was abandoned.

And since he did not take care of himself, he would probably have starved to death, had not the neighbors brought him
food in fear of something that they sensed but vaguely. The food
was brought to him by children; they were not afraid of Lazarus, nor did they mock him with naive cruelty, as children are
wont to do with the wretched and miserable. They were indifferent to him, and Lazarus answered them with the same coldness:
he had no desire to caress the black little curls, and to look into
their innocent shining eyes. Given to Time and to the Desert, his
house was crumbling down, and long since had his famishing

lowing goats wandered away to the neighboring pastures. And
his bridal garments became threadbare. Ever since that happy
day, when the musicians played, he had worn them unaware of
the difference of the new and the worn. The bright colors grew
dull and faded; vicious dogs and the sharp thorn of the Desert
turned the tender fabric into rags.

By day, when the merciless sun slew all things alive, and
even scorpions sought shelter under stones and writhed there in
a mad desire to sting, he sat motionless under the sunrays, his
blue face and the uncouth, bushy beard lifted up, bathing in
the fiery flood.

When people still talked to him, he was once asked:

"Poor Lazarus, does it please thee to sit thus and to stare
at the sun?"

And he had answered:

"Yes, it does."

So strong, it seemed, was the cold of his three-days' grave,
so deep the darkness, that there was no heat on earth to warm
Lazarus, nor a splendor that could brighten the darkness of his
eyes. That is what came to the mind of those who spoke to
Lazarus, and with a sigh they left him.

And when the scarlet, flattened globe would lower, Lazarus
would set out for the desert and walk straight toward the sun,
as though striving to reach it. He always walked straight toward the sun and those who tried to follow him and to spy
upon what he was doing at night in the desert, retained in their
memory the black silhouette of a tall stout man against the red
background of an enormous flattened disc. Night pursued
them with her horrors, and so they did not learn of Lazarus'
doings in the desert, but the vision of the black on red was forever branded on their brain. Just as a beast with a splinter in
its eye furiously rubs its muzzle with its paws, so they too fool-
ishly rubbed their eyes, but what Lazarus had given was in-
delible. and Death alone could efface it.

But there were people who lived far away, who never saw
Lazarus and knew of him only by report. With daring curiosity,
which is stronger than fear and feeds upon it, with hidden
mockery, they would come to Lazarus who was sitting in the sun
and enter into conversation with him. By this time Lazarus' appearance had changed for the better and was not so terrible.
The first minute they snapped their fingers and thought of how
stupid the inhabitants of the holy city were; but when the short
talk was over and they started homeward, their looks were such
that the inhabitants of the holy city recognized them at once
and said:

"Look, there is one more fool on whom Lazarus has set his
eye,"—and they shook their heads regretfully, and lifted up
their arms.

There came brave, intrepid warriors, with tinkling weapons;
happy youths came with laughter and song; busy tradesmen,
jingling their money, ran in for a moment, and haughty priests
leaned their crosiers against Lazarus' door, and they were all
strangely changed, as they came back. The same terrible shadow
swooped down upon their souls and gave a new appearance to
the old familiar world.

Those who still had the desire to speak, expressed their feelings thus:

"All things tangible and visible grew hollow, light and
transparent,—similar to lightsome shadows in the darkness of
night;

"for, that great darkness, which holds the whole cosmos,
was dispersed neither by the sun nor by the moon and the stars,
but like an immense black shroud enveloped the earth and, like a
mother, embraced it;

"it penetrated all the bodies, iron and stone,—and the particles of the bodies, having lost their ties, grew lonely; and it
penetrated into the depth of the particles, and the particles of
particles became lonely;

"for that great void, which encircles the cosmos, was not filled by things visible: neither by the sun, nor by the moon and the stars, but reigned unrestrained, penetrating everywhere, severing body from body, particle from particle;

"in the void hollow trees spread hollow roots, threatening a fantastic fall; temples, palaces and horses loomed up, and they were hollow; and in the void men moved about restlessly, but they were light and hollow like shadows;

"for, Time was no more, and the beginning of all things came near their end: the building was still being built, and builders were still hammering away, and its ruins were already seen and the void in its place; the man was still being born, but already funeral candles were burning at his head, and now they were extinguished, and there was the void in place of the man and of the funeral candles.

"and wrapped by void and darkness the man in despair trembled in the face of the Horror of the Infinite."

Thus spake the men who had still a desire to speak. But, surely, much more could have told those who wished not to speak, and died in silence.

IV

At that time there lived in Rome a renowned sculptor. In clay, marble and bronze he wrought bodies of gods and men, and such was their beauty, that people called them immortal. But he himself was discontented and asserted that there was something even more beautiful, that he could not embody either in marble or in bronze. "I have not yet gathered the glimmers of the moon, nor have I my fill of sunshine," he was wont to say, "and there is no soul in my marble, no life in my beautiful bronze." And when on moonlight nights he slowly walked along the road, crossing the black shadows of cypresses, his white tunic glittering in the moonshine, those who met him would laugh in a friendly way and say:

"Art thou going to gather moonshine, Aurelius? Why then didst thou not fetch baskets?"

And he would answer, laughing and pointing to his eyes:

"Here are the baskets wherein I gather the sheen of the moon and the glimmer of the sun."

And so it was: the moon glimmered in his eyes and the sun sparkled therein. But he could not translate them into marble and therein lay the serene tragedy of his life.

He was descended from an ancient patrician race, had a good wife and children, and suffered from no want.

When the obscure rumor about Lazarus reached him, he consulted his wife and friends and undertook the far journey to Judea to see him who had miraculously risen from the dead. He was somewhat weary in those days and he hoped that the road would sharpen his blunted senses. What was said of Lazarus did not frighten him: he had pondered much over Death, did not like it, but he disliked also those who confused it with life.

"In this life,—life and beauty;
beyond,—Death, the enigmatical"—

thought he, and there is no better thing for a man to do than to delight in life and in the beauty of all things living. He had even a vain glorious desire to convince Lazarus of the truth of his own view and restore his soul to life, as his body had been restored. This seemed so much easier because the rumors, shy and strange, did not render the whole truth about Lazarus and but vaguely warned against something frightful.

Lazarus had just risen from the stone in order to follow the sun which was setting in the desert, when a rich Roman attended by an armed slave, approached him and addressed him in a sonorous tone of voice:

"Lazarus!"

And Lazarus beheld a superb face, lit with glory, and arrayed in fine clothes, and precious stones sparkling in the sun.

The red light lent to the Roman's face and head the appearance of gleaming bronze — that also Lazarus noticed. He resumed obediently his place and lowered his weary eyes.

"Yes, thou art ugly, my poor Lazarus,"—quietly said the Roman, playing with his golden chain; "thou art even horrible, my poor friend; and Death was not lazy that day when thou didst fall so heedlessly into his hands. But thou art stout, and, as the great Caesar used to say, fat people are not ill-tempered; to tell the truth, I don't understand why men fear thee. Permit me to spend the night in thy house; the hour is late, and I have no shelter."

Never had anyone asked Lazarus' hospitality.

"I have no bed," said he.

"I am somewhat of a soldier and I can sleep sitting," the Roman answered. "We shall build a fire."

"I have no fire."

"Then we shall have our talk in the darkness, like two friends. I think, thou wilt find a bottle of wine."

"I have no wine."

The Roman laughed.

"Now I see why thou art so somber and dislikest thy second life. No wine! Why, then we shall do without it: there are words that make the head go round better than the Falernian."

By a sign he dismissed the slave, and they remained all alone. And again the sculptor started speaking, but it was as if, together with the setting sun, life had left his words; and they grew pale and hollow, as if they staggered on unsteady feet, as if they slipped and fell down, drunk with the heavy lees of weariness and despair. And black chasms grew up between the words — like far-off hints of the great void and the great darkness.

"Now I am thy guest, and thou wilt not be unkind to me, Lazarus!"—said he. "Hospitality is the duty even of those who for three days were dead. Three days, I was told, thou didst rest

in the grave. There it must be cold . . . and that is whence
comes thy ill habit of going without fire and wine. As to me, I
like fire; it grows dark here so rapidly. . . . The lines of thy
eyebrows and forehead are quite, quite interesting: they are like
ruins of strange palaces, buried in ashes after an earthquake.
But why dost thou wear such ugly and queer garments? I have
seen bridegrooms in thy country, and they wear such clothes —
are they not funny — and terrible. . . . But art thou a bridegroom?''

The sun had already disappeared, a monstrous black shadow
came running from the east — it was as if gigantic bare feet
began rumbling on the sand, and the wind sent a cold wave along
the backbone.

''In the darkness thou seemest still larger, Lazarus, as if
thou hast grown stouter in these moments. Dost thou feed on
darkness, Lazarus? I would fain have a little fire — at least a
little fire, a little fire. I feel somewhat chilly, your nights are so
barbarously cold. . . . Were it not so dark, I should say that
thou wert looking at me, Lazarus. Yes, it seems to me, thou art
looking. . . . Why, thou art looking at me, I feel it,—but there
thou art smiling.''

Night came, and filled the air with heavy blackness.

''How well it will be, when the sun will rise to-morrow
anew. . . . I am a great sculptor, thou knowest; that is how my
friends call me. I create. Yes, that is the word . . . but I need
daylight. I give life to the cold marble, I melt sonorous bronze
in fire, in bright hot fire. . . . Why didst thou touch me with
thy hand?''

''Come''—said Lazarus—''Thou art my guest.''

And they went to the house. And a long night enveloped
the earth.

The slave, seeing that his master did not come, went to seek
him, when the sun was already high in the sky. And he beheld
his master side by side with Lazarus: in profound silence were

they sitting right under the dazzling and scorching sunrays and looking upward. The slave began to weep and cried out:

"My master, what has befallen thee, master?"

The very same day the sculptor left for Rome. On the way Aurelius was pensive and taciturn, staring attentively at everything — the men, the ship, the sea, as though trying to retain something. On the high sea a storm burst upon them, and all through it Aurelius stayed on the deck and eagerly scanned the seas looming near and sinking with a thud.

At home his friends were frightened at the change which had taken place in Aurelius, but he calmed them, saying meaningly:

"I have found it."

And without changing the dusty clothes he wore on his journey, he fell to work, and the marble obediently resounded under his sonorous hammer. Long and eagerly worked he, admitting no one, until one morning he announced that the work was ready and ordered his friends to be summoned, severe critics and connoisseurs of art. And to meet them he put on bright and gorgeous garments, that glittered with yellow gold — and — scarlet byssus.

"Here is my work," said he thoughtfully.

His friends glanced and a shadow of profound sorrow covered their faces. It was something monstrous, deprived of all the lines and shapes familiar to the eye, but not without a hint at some new, strange image.

On a thin, crooked twig, or rather on an ugly likeness of a twig rested askew a blind, ugly, shapeless, outspread mass of something utterly and inconceivably distorted, a mad heap of wild and bizarre fragments, all feebly and vainly striving to part from one another. And, as if by chance, beneath one of the wildly-rent salients a butterfly was chiseled with divine skill, all airy loveliness, delicacy and beauty, with transparent wings, which seemed to tremble with an impotent desire to take flight.

"Wherefore this wonderful butterfly, Aurelius?" said somebody falteringly.

"I know not"—was the sculptor's answer.

But it was necessary to tell the truth, and one of his friends who loved him best said firmly:

"This is ugly, my poor friend. It must be destroyed. Give me the hammer."

And with two strokes he broke the monstrous man into pieces, leaving only the infinitely delicate butterfly untouched.

From that time on Aurelius created nothing. With profound indifference he looked at marble and bronze, and on his former divine works, where everlasting beauty rested. With the purpose of arousing his former fervent passion for work and awakening his deadened soul, his friends took him to see other artists' beautiful works,—but he remained indifferent as before, and the smile did not warm up his tightened lips. And only after listening to lengthy talks about beauty, he would retort wearily and indolently:

"But all this is a lie."

And by the day, when the sun was shining, he went into his magnificent, skillfully-built garden and having found a place without shadow, he exposed his bare head to the glare and heat. Red and white butterflies fluttered around; from the crooked lips of a drunken satyr, water streamed down with a splash into a marble cistern, but he sat motionless and silent,— like a pallid reflection of him who, in the far-off distance, at the very gates of the stony desert, sat under the fiery sun.

V

And now it came to pass that the great, deified Augustus himself summoned Lazarus. The imperial messengers dressed him gorgeously, in solemn nuptial clothes, as if Time had legalized them, and he was to remain until his very death the bridegroom of an unknown bride. It was as though an old, rotting coffin had been gilt and furnished with new, gay tassels. And men, all in trim and bright attire, rode after him, as if in bridal procession indeed, and those foremost trumpeted loudly, bidding people to clear the way for the emperor's messengers. But Lazarus' way was deserted: his native land cursed the hateful name of him who had miraculously risen from the dead, and people scattered at the very news of his appalling approach. The solitary voice of the brass trumpets sounded in the motionless air, and the wilderness alone responded with its languid echo.

Then Lazarus went by sea. And his was the most magnificently arrayed and the most mournful ship that ever mirrored itself in the azure waves of the Mediterranean Sea. Many were the travelers aboard, but like a tomb was the ship, all silence and stillness, and the despairing water sobbed at the steep, proudly curved prow. All alone sat Lazarus exposing his head to the blaze of the sun, silently listening to the murmur and splash of the wavelets, and afar seamen and messengers were sitting, a vague group of weary shadows. Had the thunder burst and the wind attacked the red sails, the ships would probably have perished, for none of those aboard had either the will or the strength to struggle for life. With a supreme effort some mariners would reach the board and eagerly scan the blue, transparent deep, hoping to see a naiad's pink shoulder flash in the hollow of an azure wave, or a drunken gay centaur dash along and in frenzy splash the wave with his hoof. But the sea was like a wilderness, and the deep was dumb and deserted.

With utter indifference did Lazarus set his feet on the street of the eternal city. As though all her wealth, all the magnificence of her palaces built by giants, all the resplendence, beauty and music of her refined life were but the echo of the wind in the wilderness, the reflection of the desert quicksand. Chariots were dashing, and along the streets were moving crowds of strong, fair, proud builders of the eternal city and haughty participants in her life; a song sounded; fountains and women laughed a pearly laughter; drunken philosophers harangued, and the sober listened to them with a smile; hoofs struck the stone pavements. And surrounded by cheerful noise, a stout, heavy man was moving, a cold spot of silence and despair, and on his way he sowed disgust, anger, and vague, gnawing weariness. Who dares to be sad in Rome, wondered indignantly the citizens, and frowned. In two days the entire city already knew all about him who had miraculously risen from the dead, and shunned him shyly.

But some daring people there were, who wanted to test their strength, and Lazarus obeyed their imprudent summons. Kept busy by state affairs, the emperor constantly delayed the reception, and seven days did he who had risen from the dead go about visiting others.

And Lazarus came to a cheerful Epicurean, and the host met him with laughter on his lips:

"Drink, Lazarus, drink!"—shouted he. "Would not Augustus laugh to see thee drunk!"

And half-naked drunken women laughed, and rose petals fell on Lazarus' blue hands. But then the Epicurean looked into Lazarus' eyes, and his gaiety ended forever. Drunkard remained he for the rest of his life; never did he drink, yet forever was he drunk. But instead of the gay revery which wine brings with it, frightful dreams began to haunt him, the sole food of his stricken spirit. Day and night he lived in the poisonous vapors of his nightmares, and death itself was not more frightful than her raving, monstrous forerunners.

And Lazarus came to a youth and his beloved, who loved each other and were most beautiful in their passion. Proudly and strongly embracing his love, the youth said with serene regret:

"Look at us, Lazarus, and share our joy. Is there anything stronger than love?"

And Lazarus looked. And for the rest of their life they kept on loving each other, but their passion grew gloomy and joyless, like those funeral cypresses whose roots feed on the decay of the graves and whose black summits in a still evening hour seek in vain to reach the sky. Thrown by the unknown forces of life into each other's embraces, they mingled tears with kisses, voluptuous pleasures with pain, and they felt themselves doubly slaves, obedient slaves to life, and patient servants of the silent Nothingness. Ever united, ever severed, they blazed like sparks and like sparks lost themselves in the boundless Dark.

And Lazarus came to a haughty sage, and the sage said to him:

"I know all the horrors thou canst reveal to me. Is there anything thou canst frighten me with?"

But before long the sage felt that the knowledge of horror was far from being the horror itself, and that the vision of Death, was not Death. And he felt that wisdom and folly are equal before the face of Infinity, for Infinity knows them not. And it vanished, the dividing-line between knowledge and ignorance, truth and falsehood, top and bottom, and the shapeless thought hung suspended in the void. Then the sage clutched his gray head and cried out frantically:

"I cannot think! I cannot think!"

Thus under the indifferent glance for him, who miraculously had risen from the dead, perished everything that asserts life, its significance and joys. And it was suggested that it was dangerous to let him see the emperor, that it was better to kill him and, having buried him secretly, to tell the emperor that he had disappeared no one knew whither. Already swords were being whetted and youths devoted to the public welfare prepared for the murder, when Augustus ordered Lazarus to be brought before him next morning, thus destroying the cruel plans.

If there was no way of getting rid of Lazarus, at least it was possible to soften the terrible impression his face produced. With this in view, skillful painters, barbers and artists were summoned, and all night long they were busy over Lazarus' head. They cropped his beard, curled it and gave it a tidy, agreeable appearance. By means of paints they concealed the corpse-like blueness of his hands and face. Repulsive were the wrinkles of suffering that furrowed his old face, and they were puttied, painted and smoothed; then, over the smooth background, wrinkles of good-tempered laughter and pleasant, carefree mirth were skillfully painted with fine brushes.

Lazarus submitted indifferently to everything that was done to him. Soon he was turned into a becomingly stout, venerable old man, into a quiet and kind grandfather of numerous offspring. It seemed that the smile, with which only a while ago he was spinning funny yarns, was still lingering on his lips, and that in the corner of his eye serene tenderness was hiding, the companion of old age. But people did not dare change his nuptial garments, and they would not change his eyes, two dark and frightful glasses through which looked at men, the unknowable Yonder.

VI

Lazarus was not moved by the magnificence of the imperial palace. It was as though he saw no difference between the crumbling house, closely pressed by the desert, and the stone palace, solid and fair, and indifferently he passed into it. And the hard marble of the floors under his feet grew similar to the quicksand of the desert, and the multitude of richly dressed and haughty men became like void air under his glance. No one looked into his face, as Lazarus passed by, fearing to fall under the appalling influence of his eyes; but when the sound of his heavy footsteps had sufficiently died down, the courtiers raised their heads and with fearful curiosity examined the figure of a stout, tall, slightly bent old man, who was slowly penetrating into the very heart of the imperial palace. Were Death itself passing, it would be faced with no greater fear: for until then the dead alone knew Death, and those alive knew Life only—and there was no bridge between them. But this extraordinary man, although alive, knew Death, and enigmatical, appalling, was his cursed knowledge. "Woe," people thought, "he will take the life of our great, deified Augustus," and they sent curses after Lazarus, who meanwhile kept on advancing into the interior of the palace.

Already did the emperor know who Lazarus was, and prepared to meet him. But the monarch was a brave man, and felt his own tremendous, unconquerable power, and in his fatal duel with him who had miraculously risen from the dead he wanted not to invoke human help. And so he met Lazarus face to face:

"Lift not thine eyes upon me, Lazarus," he ordered. "I heard thy face is like that of Medusa and turns into stone whomsoever thou lookest at. Now, I wish to see thee and to have a talk with thee, before I turn into stone,"—added he in a tone of kingly jesting, not devoid of fear.

Coming close to him, he carefully examined Lazarus' face and his strange festal garments. And although he had a keen eye, he was deceived by his appearance.

"So. Thou dost not appear terrible, my venerable old man. But the worse for us, if horror assumes such a respectable and pleasant air. Now, let us have a talk."

Augustus sat, and questioning Lazarus with his eye as much as with words, started the conversation:

"Why didst thou not greet me as thou enteredst?"

Lazarus answered indifferent:

"I knew not it was necessary."

"Art thou a Christian?"

"No."

Augustus approvingly shook his head.

"That is good. I do not like Christians. They shake the tree of life before it is covered with fruit, and disperse its odorous bloom to the winds. But who art thou?"

With a visible effort Lazarus answered:

"I was dead."

"I had heard that. But who art thou now?"

Lazarus was silent, but at last repeated in a tone of weary apathy:

"I was dead."

"Listen to me, stranger," said the emperor, distinctly and severely giving utterance to the thought that had come to him at the beginning, "my realm is the realm of Life, my people are of the living, not of the dead. Thou art here one too many. I know not who thou art and what thou sawest there; but, if thou liest, I hate thy lies, and if thou tellst the truth, I hate thy truth. In my bosom I feel the throb of life; I feel strength in my arm, and my proud thoughts, like eagles, pierce the space. And yonder in the shelter of my rule, under the protection of laws created by me, people live and toil and rejoice. Dost thou hear the battle-cry, the challenge men throw into the face of the future?"

Augustus, as in prayer, stretched forth his arms and exclaimed solemnly:

"Be blessed, O great and divine Life!"

Lazarus was silent, and with growing sternness the emperor went on:

"Thou art not wanted here, miserable remnant, snatched from under Death's teeth, thou inspirest weariness and disgust with life; like a caterpillar in the fields, thou gloatest on the rich ear of joy and belchest out the drivel of despair and sorrow. Thy truth is like a rusty sword in the hands of a nightly murderer,—and as a murderer thou shalt be executed. But before that, let me look into thine eyes. Perchance, only cowards are afraid of them, but in the brave they awake the thirst for strife and victory; then thou shalt be rewarded, not executed. . . . Now, look at me, Lazarus.''

At first it appeared to the deified Augustus that a friend was looking at him,—so soft, so tenderly-fascinating was Lazarus' glance. It promised not horror, but sweet rest, and the Infinite seemed to him a tender mistress, a compassionate sister, a mother. But stronger and stronger grew its embraces, and already the mouth, greedy of hissing kisses, interfered with the monarch's breathing, and already to the surface of the soft tissues of the body came the iron of the bones and tightened its merciless circle,—and unknown fangs, blunt and cold, touched his heart and sank into it with slow indolence.

"It pains,'' said the deified Augustus, growing pale. "But look at me, Lazarus, look.''

It was as though some heavy gates, ever closed, were slowly moving apart, and through the growing interstice the appalling horror of the Infinite poured in slowly and steadily. Like two shadows there entered the shoreless void and the unfathomable darkness; they extinguished the sun, ravished the earth from under the feet, and the roof from over the head. No more did the frozen heart ache.

"Look, look, Lazarus,'' ordered Augustus tottering.

Time stood still, and the beginning of each thing grew frightfully near to its end. Augustus' throne just erected, crumbled down, and the void was already in the place of the throne and of Augustus. Noiselessly did Rome crumble down, and a new city stood on its site and it too was swallowed by the void. Like fantastic giants, cities, states and countries fell down and vanished in the void darkness—and with uttermost indifference did the insatiable black womb of the Infinite swallow them.

"Halt!"—ordered the emperor.

In his voice sounded already a note of indifference, his hands dropped in languor, and in the vain struggle with the onrushing darkness his fiery eyes now blazed up, and now went out.

"My life thou hast taken from me, Lazarus,"—said he in a spiritless, feeble voice.

And these words of hopelessness saved him. He remembered his people, whose shield he was destined to be, and keen salutary pain pierced his deadened heart. "They are doomed to death," he thought wearily, "Serene shadows in the darkness of the Infinite," thought he, and horror grew upon him. "Frail vessels with living seething blood, with a heart that knows sorrow and also great joy," said he in his heart, and tenderness pervaded it.

Thus pondering and oscillating between the poles of Life and Death, he slowly came back to life, to find in its suffering and in its joys a shield against the darkness of the void and the horror of the Infinite.

"No, thou hast not murdered me, Lazarus," said he firmly, "but I will take thy life. Be gone."

That evening the deified Augustus partook of his meats and drinks with particular joy. Now and then his lifted hand remained suspended in the air, and a dull glimmer replaced the bright sheen of his fiery eye. It was the cold wave of Horror that surged at his feet. Defeated, but not undone, ever awaiting its hour, that Horror stood at the emperor's bedside, like a black shadow all through his life; it swayed his nights, but yielded the days to the sorrows and joys of life.

The following day, the hangman with a hot iron burnt out Lazarus' eyes. Then he was sent home. The deified Augustus dared not kill him.

*   *   *   *   *   *

Lazarus returned to the desert, and the wilderness met him with hissing gusts of wind and the heat of the blazing sun. Again he was sitting on a stone, his rough, bushy beard lifted up; and the two black holes in place of his eyes looked at the sky with an expression of dull terror. Afar-off the holy city stirred noisily and restlessly, but around him everything was deserted and dumb. No one approached the place where lived he who had miraculously risen from the dead, and long since his neighbors had forsaken their houses. Driven by the hot iron into the depth of his skull, his cursed knowledge hid there in an ambush. As though leaping out from an ambush it plunged its thousand invisible eyes into the man,—and no one dared look at Lazarus.

And in the evening, when the sun, reddening and growing wider, would come nearer and nearer the western horizon, the blind Lazarus would slowly follow it. He would stumble against stones and fall, stout and weak as he was; would rise heavily to his feet and walk on again; and on the red screen of the sunset his black body and outspread hands would form a monstrous likeness of a cross.

And it came to pass that once he went out and did not come back. Thus seemingly ended the second life of him who for three days had been under the enigmatical sway of death, and rose miraculously from the dead.

The Gentleman from San Francisco

By Ivan Bunin

"Alas, alas, that great city Babylon, that mighty city!"—
—Revelation of St. John.

THE Gentleman from San Francisco—neither at Naples nor on Capri could any one recall his name—with his wife and daughter, was on his way to Europe, where he intended to stay for two whole years, solely for the pleasure of it.

He was firmly convinced that he had a full right to a rest, enjoyment, a long comfortable trip, and what not. This conviction had a two-fold reason: first he was rich, and second, despite his fifty-eight years, he was just about to enter the stream of life's pleasures. Until now he had not really lived, but simply existed, to be sure—fairly well, yet putting off his fondest hopes for the future. He toiled unweariedly—the Chinese, whom he imported by thousands for his works, knew full well what it meant,—and finally he saw that he had made much, and that he had nearly come up to the level of those whom he had once taken as a model, and he decided to catch his breath. The class of people to which he belonged was in the habit of beginning its enjoyment of life with a trip to Europe, India, Egypt. He made up his mind to do the same. Of course, it was first of all himself that he desired to reward for the years of toil, but he was also glad for his wife and daughter's sake. His wife was never distinguished by any extraordinary impressionability, but then, all elderly American women are ardent travelers. As for his daughter, a girl of marriageable age, and somewhat sickly,—travel was the very thing she needed. Not to speak of the benefit to her health, do not happy meetings occur during travels? Abroad, one may chance to sit at the same table with a prince, or examine frescoes side by side with a multi-millionaire.

The itinerary the Gentleman from San Francisco planned out was an extensive one. In December and January he expected to relish the sun of southern Italy, monuments of antiquity, the tarantella, serenades of wandering minstrels, and that which at his age is felt most keenly—the love, not entirely disinterested though, of young Neapolitan girls. The Carnival days he planned to spend at Nice and Monte-Carlo, which at that time of the year is the meeting-place of the choicest society, the society upon which depend all the blessings of civilization: the cut of dress suits, the stability of thrones, the declaration of wars, the prosperity of hotels. Some of these people passionately give themselves over to automobile and boat races, others to roulette, others, again, busy themselves with what is called flirtation, and others shoot pigeons, which soar so beautifully from the dove-cote, hover a while over the emerald lawn, on the background of the forget-me-not colored sea, and then suddenly hit the ground, like little white lumps. Early March he wanted to devote to Florence, and at Easter, to hear the Miserere in Paris. His plans also included Venice, Paris, bull-baiting at Seville, bathing on the British Islands, also Athens, Constantinople, Palestine, Egypt, and even Japan, of course, on the way back. . . And at first things went very well indeed.

It was the end of November, and all the way to Gibraltar the ship sailed across seas which were either clad by icy darkness or swept by storms carrying wet snow. But there were no accidents, and the vessel did not even roll. The passengers,—all people of consequence—were numerous, and the steamer the famous "Atlantis," resembled the most expensive European hotel with all improvements: a night refreshment-bar, Oriental baths, even a newspaper of its own. The manner of living was a most aristocratic one; passengers rose early, awakened by the shrill voice of a bugle, filling the corridors at the gloomy hour when the day broke slowly and sulkily over the grayish-green watery desert, which rolled heavily in the fog. After putting on their flannel pajamas, they took coffee, chocolate, cocoa; they seated themselves in marble baths, went through their exercises, whetting their appetites and increasing their sense of well-being, dressed for the day, and had their breakfast. Till eleven o'clock they were supposed to stroll on the deck, breathing in the chill freshness of the ocean, or they played table-tennis, or other games which arouse the appetite. At eleven o'clock a collation was served consisting of sandwiches and bouillon, after which people read their newspapers, quietly waiting for luncheon, which was more nourishing and varied than the breakfast. The next two hours were given to rest; all the decks were crowded then with steamer chairs, on which the passengers, wrapped in plaids, lay stretched, dozing lazily, or watching the cloudy sky and the foamy-fringed water hillocks flashing beyond the sides of the vessel. At five o'clock, refreshed and gay, they drank strong, fragrant tea; at seven the sound of the bugle announced a dinner of nine courses. . . Then the Gentleman from San Francisco, rubbing his hands in an onrush of vital energy, hastened to his luxurious state-room to dress.

In the evening, all the decks of the "Atlantis" yawned in the darkness, shone with their innumerable fiery eyes, and a multitude of servants worked with increased feverishness in the kitchens, dish-washing compartments, and wine-cellars. The ocean, which heaved about the sides of the ship, was dreadful, but no one thought of it. All had faith in the controlling power of the captain, a red-headed giant, heavy and very sleepy, who, clad in a uniform with broad golden stripes, looked like a huge idol, and but rarely emerged, for the benefit of the public, from his mysterious retreat. On the fore-castle, the siren gloomily roared or screeched in a fit of mad rage, but few of the diners heard the siren: its hellish voice was covered by the sounds of an

excellent string orchestra, which played ceaselessly and exquis-
itely in a vast hall, decorated with marble and spread with vel-
vety carpets. The hall was flooded with torrents of light, radiated by crystal lustres and gilt chandeliers; it was filled with a
throng of bejeweled ladies in low-necked dresses, of men in din-
ner-coats, graceful waiters, and deferential maîtres-d'hôtel.
One of these,—who accepted wine orders exclusively—wore a
chain on his neck like some lord-mayor. The evening dress,
and the ideal linen made the Gentleman from San Francisco
look very young. Dry-skinned, of average height, strongly,
though irregularly built, glossy with thorough washing and
cleaning, and moderately animated, he sat in the golden splendor of this palace. Near him stood a bottle of amber-colored
Johannisberg, and goblets of most delicate glass and of varied
sizes, surmounted by a frizzled bunch of fresh hyacinths.
There was something Mongolian in his yellowish face with its
trimmed silvery moustache; his large teeth glimmered with
gold fillings, and his strong, bald head had a dull glow, like old
ivory. His wife, a big, broad and placid woman, was dressed
richly, but in keeping with her age. Complicated, but light,
transparent, and innocently immodest was the dress of his
daughter, tall and slender, with magnificent hair gracefully
combed; her breath was sweet with violet-scented tablets, and
she had a number of tiny and most delicate pink dimples near
her lips and between her slightly-powdered shoulder blades. . .
      The dinner lasted two whole hours, and was followed by
dances in the dancing hall, while the men—the Gentleman from
San Francisco among them—made their way to the refreshment
bar, where negros in red jackets and with eye-balls like shelled
hard-boiled eggs, waited on them. There, with their feet on
tables, smoking Havana cigars, and drinking themselves purple
in the face, they settled the destinies of nations on the basis of
the latest political and stock-exchange news. Outside, the ocean
tossed up black mountains with a thud; and the snowstorm hissed

furiously in the rigging grown heavy with slush; the ship trembled in every limb, struggling with the storm and ploughing with difficulty the shifting and seething mountainous masses that threw far and high their foaming tails; the siren groaned in agony, choked by storm and fog; the watchmen in their towers froze and almost went out of their minds under the superhuman stress of attention. Like the gloomy and sultry mass of the inferno, like its last, ninth circle, was the submersed womb of the steamer, where monstrous furnaces yawned with red-hot open jaws, and emitted deep, hooting sounds, and where the stokers, stripped to the waist, and purple with the reflected flames, bathed in their own dirty, acid sweat. And here, in the refreshment-bar, carefree men, with their feet, encased in dancing shoes, on the table, sipped cognac and liqueurs, swam in waves of spiced smoke, and exchanged subtle remarks, while in the dancing-hall everything sparkled and radiated light, warmth and joy. The couples now turned around in a waltz, now swayed in the tango; and the music, sweetly shameless and sad, persisted in its ceaseless entreaties . . . There were many persons of note in this magnificent crowd; an ambassador, a dry, modest old man; a great millionaire, shaved, tall, of an indefinite age, who, in his old-fashioned dress-coat, looked like a prelate; also a famous Spanish writer, and an international belle, already slightly faded and of dubious morals. There was also among them a loving pair, exquisite and refined, whom everybody watched with curiosity and who did not conceal their bliss; he danced only with her, sang—with great skill—only to her accompaniment, and they were so charming, so graceful. The captain alone knew that they had been hired by the company at a good salary to play at love, and that they had been sailing now on one, now on another steamer, for quite a long time.

In Gibraltar everybody was gladdened by the sun, and by the weather which was like early Spring. A new passenger appeared aboard the "Atlantis" and aroused everybody's interest. It was the crown-prince of an Asiatic state, who traveled incognito, a small man, very nimble, though looking as if made of wood, broad-faced, narrow-eyed, in gold-rimmed glasses, somewhat disagreeable because of his long black moustache, which was sparse like that of a corpse, but otherwise—charming, plain, modest. In the Mediterranean the breath of winter was again felt. The seas were heavy and motley like a peacock's tail and the waves stirred up by the gay gusts of the tramontane, tossed their white crests under a sparkling and perfectly clear sky. Next morning, the sky grew paler and the skyline misty. Land was near. Then Ischia and Capri came in sight, and one could descry, through an opera-glass, Naples, looking like pieces of sugar strewn at the foot of an indistinct dove-colored mass, and above them, a snow-covered chain of distant mountains. The decks were crowded, many ladies and gentlemen put on light fur-coats; Chinese servants, bandy-legged youths—with pitch black braids down to the heels and with girlish, thick eye-lashes,—always quiet and speaking in a whisper, were carrying to the foot of the staircases, plaid wraps, canes, and crocodile-leather valises and hand-bags. The daughter of the Gentleman from San Francisco stood near the prince, who, by a happy chance, had been introduced to her the evening before, and feigned to be looking steadily at something far-off, which he was pointing out to her, while he was, at the same time, explaining something, saying something rapidly and quietly. He was so small that he looked like a boy among other men, and he was not handsome at all. And then there was something strange about him; his glasses, derby and coat were most commonplace, but there was something horse-like in the hair of his sparse moustache, and the thin, tanned skin of his flat face looked as though it were somewhat stretched and varnished. But the girl listened to him, and so great was her excitement that she could hardly grasp the meaning of his words, her heart palpitated with incomprehensible rapture and with pride that he was standing and speaking with her and nobody else. Everything about him was different: his dry hands, his clean skin, under which flowed ancient kingly blood, even his light shoes and his European dress, plain, but singularly tidy—everything hid an inexplicable fascination and engendered thoughts of love. And the Gentleman from San Francisco, himself, in a silk-hat, gray leggings, patent leather shoes, kept eyeing the famous beauty who was standing near him, a tall, stately blonde, with eyes painted according to the latest Parisian fashion, and a tiny, bent peeled-off pet-dog, to whom she addressed herself. And the daughter, in a kind of vague perplexity, tried not to notice him.

Like all wealthy Americans he was very liberal when traveling, and believed in the complete sincerity and good-will of those who so painstakingly fed him, served him day and night, anticipating his slightest desire, protected him from dirt and disturbance, hauled things for him, hailed carriers, and delivered his luggage to hotels. So it was everywhere, and it had to be so at Naples. Meanwhile, Naples grew and came nearer. The musicians, with their shining brass instruments had already formed a group on the deck, and all of a sudden deafened everybody with the triumphant sounds of a ragtime march. The giant captain, in his full uniform appeared on the bridge and like a gracious Pagan idol, waved his hands to the passengers,— and it seemed to the Gentleman from San Francisco,—as it did to all the rest,—that for him alone thundered the march, so greatly loved by proud America, and that him alone did the captain congratulate on the safe arrival. And when the "Atlantis" had finally entered the port and all its many-decked mass leaned against the quay, and the gang-plank began to rattle heavily,—what a crowd of porters, with their assistants, in caps with golden galloons, what a crowd of various boys and husky ragamuffins with pads of colored postal cards attacked the Gentleman from San Francisco, offering their services! With kindly contempt he grinned at these beggars, and, walking

towards the automobile of the hotel where the prince might
stop, muttered between his teeth, now in English, now in
Italian—"Go away! Via . . ."

Immediately, life at Naples began to follow a set routine.
Early in the morning breakfast was served in the gloomy din-
ing-room, swept by a wet draught from the open windows looking upon a stony garden, while outside the sky was cloudy and
cheerless, and a crowd of guides swarmed at the door of the
vestibule. Then came the first smiles of the warm roseate sun,
and from the high suspended balcony, a broad vista unfolded
itself: Vesuvius, wrapped to its base in radiant morning vapors; the pearly ripple, touched to silver, of the bay, the delicate
outline of Capri on the skyline; tiny asses dragging two-
wheeled buggies along the soft, sticky embankment, and de-
tachments of little soldiers marching somewhere to the tune of
cheerful and defiant music.

Next on the day's program was a slow automobile ride along
crowded, narrow, and damp corridors of streets, between high,
many-windowed buildings. It was followed by visits to museums, lifelessly clean and lighted evenly and pleasantly, but as
though with the dull light cast by snow; — then to churches,
cold, smelling of wax, always alike: a majestic entrance, closed
by a ponderous, leather curtain, and inside—a vast void, silence,
quiet flames of seven-branched candlesticks, sending forth a red
glow from where they stood at the farther end, on the bedecked
altar,—a lonely, old woman lost among the dark wooden benches,
slippery gravestones under the feet, and somebody's "Descent
from the Cross," infallibly famous. At one o'clock—luncheon,
on the mountain of San-Martius, where at noon the choicest
people gathered, and where the daughter of the Gentleman from
San Francisco once almost fainted with joy, because it seemed to
her that she saw the Prince in the hall, although she had learned
from the newspapers that he had temporarily left for Rome. At
five o'clock it was customary to take tea at the hotel, in a smart

salon, where it was far too warm because of the carpets and the blazing fireplaces; and then came dinner-time—and again did the mighty, commanding voice of the gong resound throughout the building, again did silk rustle and the mirrors reflect files of ladies in low-necked dresses ascending the staircases, and again the splendid palatial dining hall opened with broad hospitality, and again the musicians' jackets formed red patches on the estrade, and the black figures of the waiters swarmed around the maître-d'hôtel, who, with extraordinary skill, poured a thick pink soup into plates . . . As everywhere, the dinner was the crown of the day. People dressed for it as for a wedding, and so abundant was it in food, wines, mineral waters, sweets and fruits, that about eleven o'clock in the evening chamber-maids would carry to all the rooms hot-water bags.

That year, however, December did not happen to be a very propitious one. The doormen were abashed when people spoke to them about the weather, and shrugged their shoulders guiltily, mumbling that they could not recollect such a year, although, to tell the truth, it was not the first year they mumbled those words, usually adding that "things are terrible everywhere": that unprecedented showers and storms had broken out on the Riviera, that it was snowing in Athens, that Aetna, too, was all blocked up with snow, and glowed brightly at night, and that tourists were fleeing from Palermo to save themselves from the cold spell . . .

That winter, the morning sun daily deceived Naples: toward noon the sky would invariably grow gray, and a light rain would begin to fall, growing thicker and duller. Then the palms at the hotel-porch glistened disagreeably like wet tin, the town appeared exceptionally dirty and congested, the museums too monotonous, the cigars of the drivers in their rubber raincoats, which flattened in the wind like wings, intolerably stinking, and the energetic flapping of their whips over their thin-necked nags —obviously false. The shoes of the signors, who cleaned the street-car tracks, were in a frightful state, the women who splashed in the mud, with black hair unprotected from the rain, were ugly and short-legged, and the humidity mingled with the foul smell of rotting fish, that came from the foaming sea, was simply disheartening. And so, early-morning quarrels began to break out between the Gentleman from San Francisco and his wife; and their daughter now grew pale and suffered from headaches, and now became animated, enthusiastic over everything, and at such times was lovely and beautiful. Beautiful were the tender, complex feelings which her meeting with the ungainly man aroused in her,—the man in whose veins flowed unusual blood, for, after all, it does not matter what in particular stirs up a maiden's soul: money, or fame, or nobility of birth . . . Everybody assured the tourists that it was quite different at Sorrento and on Capri, that lemon-trees were blossoming there, that it was warmer and sunnier there, the morals purer, and the wine less adulterated. And the family from San Francisco decided to set out with all their luggage for Capri. They planned to settle down at Sorrento, but first to visit the island, tread the stones where stood Tiberius's palaces, examine the fabulous wonders of the Blue Grotto, and listen to the bagpipes of Abruzzi, who roam about the island during the whole month preceding Christmas and sing the praises of the Madona.

On the day of departure—a very memorable day for the family from San Francisco—the sun did not appear even in the morning. A heavy winter fog covered Vesuvius down to its very base and hung like a gray curtain low over the leaden surge of the sea, hiding it completely at a distance of half a mile. Capri was completely out of sight, as though it had never existed on this earth. And the little steamboat which was making for the island tossed and pitched so fiercely that the family lay prostrated on the sofas in the miserable cabin of the little steamer, with their feet wrapped in plaids and their eyes shut because of their nausea. The older lady suffered, as she thought, most; several times she was overcome with sea-sickness, and it seemed to her then she was dying, but the chambermaid, who repeatedly brought her the basin, and who for many years, in heat and in cold, had been tossing on these waves, ever on the alert, ever kindly to all,—the chambermaid only laughed. The lady's daughter was frightfully pale and kept a slice of lemon between her teeth. Not even the hope of an unexpected meeting with the prince at Sorrento, where he planned to arrive on Christmas, served to cheer her. The Gentleman from San Francisco, who was lying on his back, dressed in a large overcoat and a big cap, did not loosen his jaws throughout the voyage. His face grew dark, his moustache white, and his head ached heavily; for the last few days, because of the bad weather, he had drunk far too much in the evenings.

And the rain kept on beating against the rattling window panes, and water dripped down from them on the sofas; the howling wind attacked the masts, and sometimes, aided by a heavy sea, it laid the little steamer on its side, and then something below rolled about with a rattle.

While the steamer was anchored at Castellamare and Sorrento, the situation was more cheerful; but even here the ship rolled terribly, and the coast with all its precipices, gardens and pines, with its pink and white hotels and hazy mountains clad in curling verdure, flew up and down as if it were on swings. The rowboats hit against the sides of the steamer, the sailors and the deck passengers shouted at the top of their voices, and somewhere a baby screamed as if it were being crushed to pieces. A wet wind blew through the door, and from a wavering barge flying the flag of the Hotel Royal, an urchin kept on unwearyingly shouting "Kgoyal-al! Hotel Kgoyal-al! . . ." inviting tourists. And the Gentleman from San Francisco felt like the old man that he was,—and it was with weariness and animosity that he thought of all these

"Royals," "Splendids," "Excelsiors," and of all those greedy bugs, reeking with garlic, who are called Italians. Once, during a stop, having opened his eyes and half-risen from the sofa, he noticed in the shadow of the rock beach a heap of stone huts, miserable, mildewed through and through, huddled close by the water, near boats, rags, tin-boxes, and brown fishing nets,—and as he remembered that this was the very Italy he had come to enjoy, he felt a great despair . . . Finally, in twilight, the black mass of the island began to grow nearer, as though burrowed through at the base by red fires, the wind grew softer, warmer, more fragrant; from the dock-lanterns huge golden serpents flowed down the tame waves which undulated like black oil . . . Then, suddenly, the anchor rumbled and fell with a splash into the water, the fierce yells of the boatman filled the air, — and at once everyone's heart grew easy. The electric lights in the cabin grew more brilliant, and there came a desire to eat, drink, smoke, move . . . Ten minutes later the family from San Francisco found themselves in a large ferry-boat; fifteen minutes later they trod the stones of the quay, and then seated themselves in a small lighted car, which, with a buzz, started to ascend the slope, while vineyard stakes, half-ruined stone fences, and wet, crooked lemon-trees, in spots shielded by straw sheds, with their glimmering orange-colored fruit and thick glossy foliage, were sliding down past the open car windows. . . After rain, the earth smells sweetly in Italy, and each of her islands has a fragrance of its own.

The Island of Capri was dark and damp on that evening. But for a while it grew animated and let up, in spots, as always in the hour of the steamer's arrival. On the top of the hill, at the station of the *funiculaire*, there stood already the crowd of those whose duty it was to receive properly the Gentleman from San Francisco. The rest of the tourists hardly deserved any attention. There were a few Russians, who had settled on Capri, untidy, absent-minded people, absorbed in their bookish thoughts, spectacled, bearded, with the collars of their cloth overcoats raised. There was also a company of long-legged, long-necked, round-headed German youths in Tyrolean costume, and with linen bags on their backs, who need no one's services, are everywhere at home, and are by no means liberal in their expenses. The Gentleman from San Francisco, who quietly kept aloof from both the Russians and the Germans, was noticed at once. He and his ladies were hurriedly helped from the car, a man ran before them to show them the way, and they were again surrounded by boys and those thickset Caprean peasant women, who carry on their heads the trunks and valises of wealthy travelers. Their tiny, wooden, foot-stools rapped against the pavement of the small square, which looked almost like an opera square, and over which an electric lantern swung in the damp wind; the gang of urchins whistled like birds and turned somersaults, and as the Gentleman from San Francisco passed among them, it all looked like a stage scene; he went first under some kind of mediaeval archway, beneath houses huddled close together, and then along a steep echoing lane which led to the hotel entrance, flooded with light. At the left, a palm tree raised its tuft above the flat roofs, and higher up, blue stars burned in the black sky. And again things looked as though it was in honor of the guests from San Francisco that the stony damp little town had awakened on its rocky island in the Mediterranean, that it was they who had made the owner of the hotel so happy and beaming, and that the Chinese gong, which had sounded the call to dinner through all the floors as soon as they entered the lobby, had been waiting only for them.

The owner, an elegant young man, who met the guests with a polite and exquisite bow, for a moment startled the Gentleman from San Francisco. Having caught sight of him, the Gentleman from San Francisco suddenly recollected that on the previous night, among other confused images which disturbed his sleep, he had seen this very man. His vision resembled the hotel keeper to a dot, had the same head, the same hair, shining and scrupulously combed, and wore the same frock-coat with rounded skirts. Amazed, he almost stopped for a while. But as there was not a mustard-seed of what is called mysticism in his heart, his surprise subsided at once; in passing the corridor of the hotel he jestingly told his wife and daughter about this strange coincidence of dream and reality. His daughter alone glanced at him with alarm, longing suddenly compressed her heart, and such a strong feeling of solitude on this strange, dark island seized her that she almost began to cry. But, as usual, she said nothing about her feelings to her father.

A person of high dignity, Rex XVII, who had spent three entire weeks on Capri, had just left the island, and the guests from San Francisco were given the apartments he had occupied. At their disposal was put the most handsome and skillful chambermaid, a Belgian, with a figure rendered slim and firm by her corset, and with a starched cap, shaped like a small, indented crown; and they had the privilege of being served by the most well-appearing and portly footman, a black, fiery-eyed Sicilian, and by the quickest waiter, the small, stout Luigi, who was a fiend at cracking jokes and had changed many places in his life. Then the maître-d'hôtel, a Frenchman, gently rapped at the door of the American gentleman's room. He came to ask whether the gentleman and the ladies would dine, and in case they would, which he did not doubt, to report that there was to be had that day lobsters, roast beef, asparagus, pheasants, etc., etc.

The floor was still rocking under the Gentleman from San Francisco—so sea-sick had the wretched Italian steamer made him—yet, he slowly, though awkwardly, shut the window which had banged when the maître-d'hôtel entered, and which let in the smell of the distant kitchen and wet flowers in the garden,

and answered with slow distinctness, that they would dine, that
their table must be placed farther away from the door, in the
depth of the hall, that they would have local wine and cham-
pagne, moderately dry and but slightly cooled. The maître-
d'hôtel approved the words of the guest in various intonations,
which all meant, however, only one thing; there is and can be
no doubt that the desires of the Gentleman from San Francisco
are right, and that everything would be carried out, in exact
conformity with his words. At last he inclined his head and
asked delicately:

"Is that all, sir?"

And having received in reply a slow "Yes," he added that
to-day they were going to have the tarantella danced in the
vestibule by Carmella and Giuseppe, known to all Italy and to
"the entire world of tourists."

"I saw her on post-card pictures," said the Gentleman
from San Francisco in a tone of voice which expressed nothing.
"And this Giuseppe, is he her husband?"

"Her cousin, sir," answered the maître-d'hôtel.

The Gentleman from San Francisco tarried a little, evidently musing on something, but said nothing, then dismissed
him with a nod of his head.

Then he started making preparations, as though for a wedding: he turned on all the electric lamps, and filled the mirrors
with reflections of light and the sheen of furniture, and opened
trunks; he began to shave and to wash himself, and the sound
of his bell was heard every minute in the corridor, crossing
with other impatient calls which came from the rooms of his
wife and daughter. Luigi, in his red apron, with the ease char-
acteristic of stout people, made funny faces at the chambermaids,
who were dashing by with tile buckets in their hands, making
them laugh until the tears came. He rolled head over heels
to the door, and, tapping with his knuckles, asked with feigned

timidity and with an obsequiousness which he knew how to render idiotic:

"Ha sonata, Signore?" (Did you ring, sir?)

And from behind the door a slow, grating, insultingly polite voice, answered:

"Yes, come in."

What did the Gentleman from San Francisco think and feel on that evening forever memorable to him? It must be said frankly: absolutely nothing exceptional. The trouble is that everything on this earth appears too simple. Even had he felt anything deep in his heart, a premonition that something was going to happen, he would have imagined that it was not going to happen so soon, at least not at once. Besides, as is usually the case just after sea-sickness is over, he was very hungry, and he anticipated with real delight the first spoonful of soup, and the first gulp of wine; therefore, he was performing the habitual process of dressing, in a state of excitement which left no time for reflection.

Having shaved and washed himself, and dexterously put in place a few false teeth, he then, standing before the mirror, moistened and vigorously plastered what was left of his thick pearly-colored hair, close to his tawny-yellow skull. Then he put on, with some effort, a tight-fitting undershirt of cream-colored silk, fitted tight to his strong, aged body with its waist swelling out because of an abundant diet; and he pulled black silk socks and patent-leather dancing shoes on his dry feet with their fallen arches. Squatting down, he set right his black trousers, drawn high by means of silk suspenders, adjusted his snow-white shirt with its bulging front, put the buttons into the shining cuffs, and began the painful process of hunting up the front button under the hard collar. The floor was still swaying under him, the tips of his fingers hurt terribly, the button at times painfully pinched the flabby skin in the depression under his Adam's apple, but he persevered, and finally, with his eyes shining from the effort, his face blue because of the narrow collar which squeezed his neck, he triumphed over the difficulties —and all exhausted, he sat down before the glass-pier, his reflected image repeating itself in all the mirrors.

"It's terrible!" he muttered, lowering his strong, bald head and making no effort to understand what was terrible; then, with a careful and habitual gesture, he examined his short fingers with gouty callosities in the joints, and their large, convex, almond-colored nails, and repeated with conviction, "It's terrible!"

But here the stentorian voice of the second gong sounded throughout the house, as in a heathen temple. And having risen hurriedly, the Gentleman from San Francisco drew his tie more taut and firm around his collar, and pulled together his abdomen by means of a tight waistcoat, put on a dinner-coat, set to rights the cuffs, and for the last time he examined himself in the mirror... This Carnella, tawny as a mulatto, with fiery eyes, in a dazzling dress in which orange-color predominated, must be an extraordinary dancer,—it occurred to him. And cheerfully leaving his room, he walked on the carpet, to his wife's chamber, and asked in a loud tone of voice if they would be long.

"In five minutes, papa!" answered cheerfully and gaily a girlish voice. "I am combing my hair."

"Very well," said the Gentleman from San Francisco.

And thinking of her wonderful hair, streaming on her shoulders, he slowly walked down along corridors and staircases, spread with red velvet carpets,—looking for the library. The servants he met hugged the walls, and he walked by as if not noticing them. An old lady, late for dinner, already bowed with years, with milk-white hair, yet bare-necked, in a light-gray silk dress, hurried at top speed, but she walked in a mincing, funny, hen-like manner, and he easily overtook her. At the glass door of the dining hall where the guests had already gathered and started eating, he stopped before the table crowded with boxes of matches and Egyptian cigarettes, took a great Manilla cigar, and threw three liras on the table. On the winter veranda he glanced into the open window; a stream of soft air came to him from the darkness, the top of the old palm loomed up before him afar-off, with its boughs spread among the stars and looking gigantic, and the distant even noise of the sea reached his ear. In the library-room, snug, quiet, a German in round silver-bowed glasses and with crazy, wondering eyes— stood turning the rustling pages of a newspaper. Having coldly eyed him, the Gentleman from San Francisco seated himself in a deep leather arm-chair near a lamp under a green hood, put on his pince-nez and twitching his head because of the collar which choked him, hid himself from view behind a newspaper. He glanced at a few headlines, read a few lines about the interminable Balkan war, and turned over the page with an habitual gesture. Suddenly, the lines blazed up with a glassy sheen, the veins of his neck swelled, his eyes bulged out, the pince-nez fell from his nose . . . He dashed forward, wanted to swallow air—and made a wild, rattling noise; his lower jaw dropped, dropped on his shoulder and began to shake, the shirt-front bulged out,—and the whole body, writhing, the heels catching in the carpet, slowly fell to the floor in a desperate struggle with an invisible foe . . .

Had not the German been in the library, this frightful accident would have been quickly and adroitly hushed up. The body of the Gentleman from San Francisco would have been rushed away to some far corner—and none of the guests would have known of the occurence. But the German dashed out of the library with outcries and spread the alarm all over the house. And many rose from their meal, upsetting chairs, others growing pale, ran along the corridors to the library, and the question, asked in many languages, was heard: "What is it? What has happened?" And no one was able to answer it clearly, no one understood anything, for until this very day men still wonder most at death and most absolutely refuse to believe in it. The owner rushed from one guest to another, trying to keep back those who were running and soothe them with hasty assurances, that this was nothing, a mere trifle, a little fainting-spell by which a Gentleman from San Francisco had been overcome. But no one listened to him, many saw how the footmen and waiters tore from the gentleman his tie, collar, waistcoat, the rumpled evening coat, and even—for no visible reason—the dancing shoes from his black silk-covered feet. And he kept on writhing. He obstinately struggled with death, he did not want to yield to the foe that attacked him so unexpectedly and grossly. He shook his head, emitted rattling sounds like one throttled, and turned up his eye-balls like one drunk with wine. When he was hastily brought into Number Forty-three,—the smallest, worst, dampest, and coldest room at the end of the lower corridor,—and stretched on the bed,—his daughter came running, her hair falling over her shoulders, the skirts of her dressing-gown thrown open, with bare breasts raised by the corset. Then came his wife, big, heavy, almost completely dressed for dinner, her mouth round with terror.

In a quarter of an hour all was again in good trim at the hotel. But the evening was irreparably spoiled. Some tourists returned to the dining-hall and finished their dinner, but they kept silent, and it was obvious that they took the accident as a personal insult, while the owner went from one guest to another, shrugging his shoulders in impotent and appropriate irritation, feeling like one innocently victimized, assuring everyone that he understood perfectly well "how disagreeable this is," and giving his word that he would take all "the measures that are within his power" to do away with the trouble. Yet it was found necessary to cancel the tarantella. The unnecessary electric lamps were put out, most of the guests left for the beer-hall, and it grew so quiet in the hotel that one could distinctly hear the tick-tock of the clock in the lobby, where a lonely parrot babbled something in its expressionless manner, stirring in its cage, and trying to fall asleep with its paw clutching the upper perch in a most absurd manner. The Gentleman from San Francisco lay stretched in a cheap iron bed, under coarse woolen blankets, dimly lighted by a single gas-burner fastened in the ceiling. An ice-bag slid down on his wet, cold forehead. His blue, already lifeless face grew gradually cold; the hoarse, rattling noise which came from his mouth, lighted by the glimmer of the golden fillings, gradually weakened. It was not the Gentleman from San Francisco that was emitting those weird sounds; he was no more,—some-one else did it. His wife and daughter, the doctor, the servants were standing and watching him apathetically. Suddenly, that which they expected and feared happened. The rattling sound ceased. And slowly, slowly, in everybody's sight a pallor stole over the face of the dead man, and his features began to grow thinner and more luminous, beautiful with the beauty that he had long shunned and that became him well . . .

The proprietor entered. "Gia e morto," whispered the doctor to him. The proprietor shrugged his shoulders indifferently. The older lady, with tears slowly running down her cheeks, approached him and said timidly that now the deceased must be taken to his room.

"O no, madam," answered the proprietor politely, but without any amiability and not in English, but in French. He was no longer interested in the trifle which the guests from San Francisco could now leave at his cash-office. "This is absolutely impossible," he said, and added in the form of an explanation that he valued this apartment highly, and if he satisfied her desire, this would become known over Capri and the tourists would begin to avoid it.

The girl, who had looked at him strangely, sat down, and with her handkerchief to her mouth, began to cry. Her mother's tears dried up at once, and her face flared up. She raised her tone, began to demand, using her own language and still unable to realize that the respect for her was absolutely gone. The proprietor, with polite dignity, cut her short: "If madam does not like the ways of this hotel, he dare not detain her." And he firmly announced that the corpse must leave the hotel that very day, at dawn, that the police had been informed, that an agent would call immediately and attend to all the necessary formalities... "Is it possible to get on Capri at least a plain coffin?" madam asks... Unfortunately not; by no means, and as for making one, there will be no time. It will be necessary to arrange things some other way... For instance, he gets English soda-water in big, oblong boxes. . . The partitions could be taken out from such a box...

By night, the whole hotel was asleep. A waiter opened the window in Number 43—it faced a corner of the garden where a consumptive banana-tree grew in the shadow of a high stone wall set with broken glass on the top—turned out the electric light, locked the door, and went away. The deceased remained alone in the darkness. Blue stars looked down at him from the black sky, the cricket in the wall started his melancholy, care-free song. In the dimly lighted corridor two chambermaids were sitting on the window-sill, mending something. Then Luigi came in, in slippered feet, with a heap of clothes on his arm.

"*Pronto?*"—he asked in a stage whisper, as if greatly concerned, directing his eyes toward the terrible door, at the end of the corridor. And waving his free hand in that direction, "*Partenza!*" he cried out in a whisper, as if seeing off a train,— and the chambermaids, choking with noiseless laughter, put their heads on each other's shoulders.

Then, stepping softly, he ran to the door, slightly rapped at it, and inclining his ear, asked most obsequiously in a subdued tone of voice:

"Ha sonata, signore?"

And, squeezing his throat and thrusting his lower jaw forward, he answered himself in a drawling, grating, sad voice, as if from behind the door:

"Yes, come in . . . ."

At dawn, when the window panes in Number Forty-three grew white, and a damp wind rustled in the leaves of the banana-tree, when the pale-blue morning sky rose and stretched over Capri, and the sun, rising from behind the distant mountains of Italy, touched into gold the pure, clearly outlined summit of Monte Solaro, when the masons, who mended the paths for the tourists on the island, went out to their work,—an oblong box was brought to room number forty-three. Soon it grew very heavy and painfully pressed against the knees of the assistant doorman who was conveying it in a one-horse carriage along the white highroad which winded on the slopes, among stone fences and vineyards, all the way down to the sea-coast. The driver, a sickly man, with red eyes, in an old short-sleeved coat and in worn-out shoes, had a drunken headache; all night long he had played dice at the eatinghouse—and he kept on flogging his vigorous little horse. According to Sicilian custom, the animal was heavily burdened with decorations: all sorts of bells tinkled on the bridle, which was ornamented with colored woolen fringes; there were bells also on the edges of the high saddle; and a bird's feather, two feet long, stuck in the trimmed crest of the horse, nodded up and down. The driver kept silence: he was depressed by his wrongheadedness and vices, by the fact that last night he had lost in gambling all the copper coins with which his pockets had been full,—neither more nor less than four liras and forty centesimi. But on such a morning, when the air is so fresh, and the sea stretches nearby, and the sky is serene with a morning serenity,—a headache passes rapidly and one becomes carefree again. Besides, the driver was also somewhat cheered by the unexpected earnings which the Gentleman from San Francisco, who bumped his dead head against the walls of the box behind his back, had brought him. The little steamer, shaped like a great bug, which lay far down, on the tender and brilliant blue filling to the brim the Neapolitan bay, was blowing the signal of departure,—and the sounds swiftly resounded all over Capri. Every bend of the island, every ridge and stone was seen as distinctly as if there were no air between heaven and earth. Near the quay the driver was overtaken by the head doorman who conducted in an auto the wife and daughter of the Gentleman from San Francisco. Their faces were pale and their eyes sunken with tears and a sleepless night. And in ten minutes the little steamer was again stirring up the water and picking its way toward Sorrento and Castellamare, carrying the American family away from Capri forever. . . . Meanwhile, peace and rest were restored on the island.

Two thousand years ago there had lived on that island a man who became utterly entangled in his own brutal and filthy actions. For some unknown reason he usurped the rule over millions of men and found himself bewildered by the absurdity of this power, while the fear that someone might kill him unawares, made him commit deeds inhuman beyond all measure. And mankind has forever retained his memory, and those who, taken together, now rule the world, as incomprehensibly and, essentially, as cruelly as he did,—come from all the corners of the earth to look at the remnants of the stone house he inhabited, which stands on one of the steepest cliffs of the island. On that wonderful morning the tourists, who had come to Capri for precisely that purpose, were still asleep in the various hotels, but tiny long-eared asses under red saddles were already being led to the hotel entrances. Americans and Germans, men and women, old and young, after having arisen and breakfasted heartily, were to scramble on them, and the old beggar-women of Capri, with sticks in their sinewy hands, were again to run after them along stony, mountainous paths, all the way up to the summit of Monte Tiberia. The dead old man from San Francisco, who had planned to keep the tourists company but who had, instead, only scared them by reminding them of death, was already shipped to Naples, and soothed by this, the travelers slept soundly, and silence reigned over the island. The stores in the little town were still closed, with the exception of the fish and greens market on the tiny square. Among the plain people who filled it, going about their business, stood idly by, as usual, Lorenzo, a tall old boatman, a carefree reveller and once a handsome man, famous all over Italy, who had many times served as a model for painters. He had brought and already sold — for a song — two big sea-crawfish, which he had caught at night and which were rustling in the apron of Don Cataldo, the cook of the hotel where the family from San Francisco had been lodged, — and now Lorenzo could stand calmly until nightfall, wearing princely airs, showing off his rags, his clay pipe with its long reed mouth-piece, and his red woolen cap, tilted on one ear. Meanwhile, among the precipices of Monte Solare, down the ancient Phoenician road, cut in the rocks in the form of a gigantic staircase, two Abruzzi mountaineers were coming from Anacapri. One carried under his leather mantle a bagpipe, a large goat's skin with two pipes; the other, something in the nature of a wooden flute. They walked, and the entire country, joyous, beautiful. sunny, stretched below them; the rocky shoulders of the island, which lay at their feet, the fabulous blue in which it swam, the shining morning vapors over the sea westward, beneath the dazzling sun, and the wavering masses of Italy's mountains, both near and distant, whose beauty human word is powerless to render. . . Midway they slowed up. Overshadowing the road stood, in a grotto of the rock wall of Monte Solare, the Holy Virgin, all radiant, bathed in the warmth and the splendor of the sun. The rust of her snow-white plaster-

of-Paris vestures and queenly crown was touched into gold, and
there were meekness and mercy in her eyes raised toward the
heavens, toward the eternal and beatific abode of her thrice-
blessed Son. They bared their heads, applied the pipes to their
lips,—and praises flowed on, candid and humbly-joyous, praises
to the sun and the morning, to Her, the Immaculate Intercessor
for all who suffer in this evil and beautiful world, and to Him
who had been born of her womb in the cavern of Bethlehem, in
a hut of lowly shepherds in distant Judea.

As for the body of the dead Gentleman from San Francisco, it was on its way home, to the shores of the New World,
where a grave awaited it. Having undergone many humilia-
tions and suffered much human neglect, having wandered about
a week from one port warehouse to another, it finally got
on that same famous ship which had brought the family, such
a short while ago and with such a pomp, to the Old World.
But now he was concealed from the living: in a tar-coated
coffin he was lowered deep into the black hold of the steamer.
And again did the ship set out on its far sea journey. At night
it sailed by the island of Capri, and, for those who watched
it from the island, its lights slowly disappearing in the dark
sea, it seemed infinitely sad. But there, on the vast steamer,
in its lighted halls shining with brilliance and marble, a noisy
dancing party was going on, as usual.

On the second and the third night there was again a ball—
this time in mid-ocean, during a furious storm sweeping over the
ocean, which roared like a funeral mass and rolled up mountainous seas fringed with mourning silvery foam. The Devil, who
from the rocks of Gibraltar, the stony gateway of two worlds,
watched the ship vanish into night and storm, could hardly
distinguish from behind the snow the innumerable fiery eyes of
the ship. The Devil was as huge as a cliff, but the ship was
even bigger, a many-storied, many-stacked giant, created by the
arrogance of the New Man with the old heart. The blizzard

battered the ship's rigging and its broad-necked stacks, whit-
ened with snow, but it remained firm, majestic—and terrible.
On its uppermost deck, amidst a snowy whirlwind there loomed
up in loneliness the cozy, dimly lighted cabin, where, only half
awake, the vessel's ponderous pilot reigned over its entire mass,
bearing the semblance of a pagan idol. He heard the wailing
moans and the furious screeching of the siren, choked by the
storm, but the nearness of that which was behind the wall and
which in the last account was incomprehensible to him, removed
his fears. He was reassured by the thought of the large, armored
cabin, which now and then was filled with mysterious rumbling
sounds and with the dry creaking of blue fires, flaring up
and exploding around a man with a metallic headpiece, who
was eagerly catching the indistinct voices of the vessels that
hailed him, hundreds of miles away. At the very bottom, in
the under-water womb of the "Atlantis," the huge masses of
tanks and various other machines, their steel parts shining
dully, wheezed with steam and oozed hot water and oil; here was
the gigantic kitchen, heated by hellish furnaces, where the mo-
tion of the vessel was being generated; here seethed those
forces terrible in their concentration which were transmitted to
the keel of the vessel, and into that endless round tunnel, which
was lighted by electricity, and looked like a gigantic cannon
barrel, where slowly, with a punctuality and certainty that
crushes the human soul, a colossal shaft was revolving in its oily
nest, like a living monster stretching in its lair. As for the
middle part of the "Atlantis," its warm, luxurious cabins,
dining-rooms, and halls, they radiated light and joy, were astir
with a chattering smartly-dressed crowd, were filled with the
fragrance of fresh flowers, and resounded with a string orchestra.
And again did the slender supple pair of hired lovers painfully
turn and twist and at times clash convulsively amid the splendor
of lights, silks, diamonds, and bare feminine shoulders: she—
a sinfully modest pretty girl, with lowered eyelashes and an

innocent hair-dressing, he—a tall, young man, with black hair, looking as if they were pasted, pale with powder, in most exquisite patent-leather shoes, in a narrow, long-skirted dress-coat,—a beautiful man resembling a leech. And no one knew that this couple has long since been weary of torturing themselves with a feigned beatific torture under the sounds of shamefully-melancholy music; nor did any one who know what lay deep, deep, beneath them, on the very bottom of the hold, in the neighborhood of the gloomy and sultry maw of the ship, that heavily struggled with the ocean, the darkness, and the storm. . .